Tomorrow's Olympian

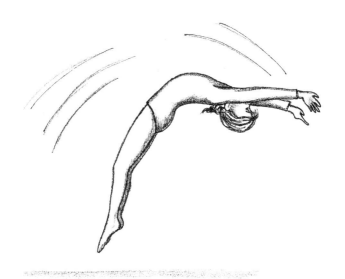

by Alison Peters

illustrated by Coralie Islip

PICTURE WINDOW BOOKS
Minneapolis, Minnesota

Editor: Jill Kalz
Page Production: Melissa Kes
Creative Director: Keith Griffin
Editorial Director: Carol Jones

First American edition published in 2006 by
Picture Window Books
5115 Excelsior Boulevard
Suite 232
Minneapolis, MN 55416
877-845-8392
www.picturewindowbooks.com

First published in Australia by
Blake Education Pty Ltd
ACN 074 266 023
Locked Bag 2022
Glebe NSW 2037
Ph: (02) 9518 4222; Fax: (02) 9518 4333
E-mail: mail@blake.com.au
www.askblake.com.au
Text copyright © 2000 Alison Peters
Illustrations copyright © 2000 Blake Education
Illustrated by Coralie Islip

Printed in the United States of America.

Library of Congress Cataloging-in-Publication Data
Peters, Alison.
Tomorrow's Olympian / by Alison Peters ; illustrated by Coralie Islip.
p. cm. — (Read-it! chapter books. Sports)
Summary: To have any hope of reaching her goal of competing in the
Olympics, Kelly must not only learn to do a back handspring on the beam,
she must also conquer her fear.
ISBN 1-4048-1665-8 (hardcover)
[1. Gymnastics—Fiction. 2. Self-confidence—Fiction.] I. Islip, Coralie, ill. II. Title.
III. Series.
PZ7.P441546Tom 2005
[Fic]—dc22   2005027157

Table of Contents

Chapter 1
Kelly's Dream

Kelly watched Annabelle throw bits of brown leaves into the lake.

"Here, ducky, ducky. Here's some yummy bread. Lunchtime," Annabelle said.

But the ducks weren't fooled. They paddled farther away from her.

"Smart birds," Kelly thought.

Quietly, she walked away from the rest of her class, along the bank of the lake. The branches of a willow hung into the water. Kelly walked underneath.

"It's like a private hideaway," she thought, "and these leaves are like curtains."

She imagined how it would feel to cartwheel through them.

Without thinking, she cartwheeled.

6

"Oh! Look, girls," said a voice, "there's 'Tomorrow's Olympian!'" It was Annabelle and her friends. "It's not enough to boast in the newspaper, is it? You have to show off on field trips, too."

Kelly felt her cheeks burn.

"I didn't think ... um ...," Kelly began. She hadn't meant to boast when the man from the newspaper asked her about her dreams. She had been interviewed for winning the regional gymnastics final.

She didn't know he would put her on the front page with "Tomorrow's Olympian" written in large letters above her head. Besides, lots of people dream about going to the Olympics.

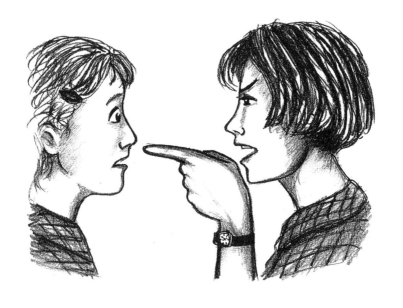

"I didn't know anyone was watching," Kelly blurted out. "I'm sorry."

"You should be," Annabelle said, pointing her finger in Kelly's face. She turned and led the others out from under the willow.

Kelly swatted at the willow branches.

"Why did I say I was sorry?" she asked herself. "Next time, I'll stand up to her. Next time, I'll ... I'll say ...."

She couldn't think of anything to say. Deep down she knew that she would never have the guts to stand up to Annabelle.

Chapter 2
Being Brave

"Guts," Kelly told her father. "I just don't have the guts."

Her dad smiled at her.

"Yes, you do," he said. "You had guts last week in the gymnastics final. You were so scared your knees were shaking. But you got up there and did it anyway. That took a lot of courage."

"That's different," said Kelly. "Annabelle wasn't there making fun of me. Besides, I'm still too scared to do a back handspring on the balance beam. So I haven't got enough guts in gymnastics, either."

"Ahhh," her dad nodded. "You're still thinking about the back handspring."

This move scared Kelly even more than Annabelle did.

"I can't stop thinking about it. If I don't learn it soon, I won't be able to move up to Level Eight," Kelly said, "and Nadia wants me to do it at the State Championship."

Nadia was Kelly's coach. "You are a natural, Kelly," Nadia would say. "Olympic material."

Kelly had to take it step by step. Getting to Level Eight was the next step. The back handspring on the beam was the only thing that stood in her way.

"There's always next year," said her dad.

"Dad, you know that's not soon enough," Kelly said. "The next Olympic Games are in four years. If I'm not a Level Ten champion, I'll have no chance of getting on the Olympic team."

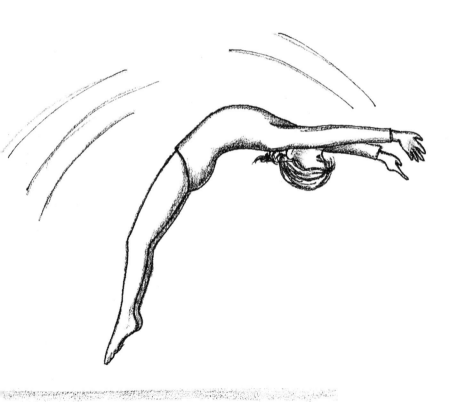

"OK then, let's not waste any more time worrying about Annabottom. I mean, Spannerbelle. Or is it Annasmell?" Kelly's dad asked, snapping his fingers.

Kelly almost choked on her dinner as she laughed. Sometimes her dad acted like a kid.

"If you really want to become an Olympic champion," he continued, "you've got more important things to think about."

Kelly shrugged.

"I guess you're right," she said.

"I'm always right," he said.

Kelly rolled her eyes.

Chapter 3
Make It Stick!

"You can do the back handspring on the ground," said Nadia at training the next day. "You've done it hundreds of times. I know you can do it on the beam."

Kelly wasn't so sure.

Once she had seen one of the older girls fall off while trying the back handspring. Her ankle had twisted as she landed.

Kelly could still remember how she cried out in pain. The bone was fractured.

"Kelly," Nadia said quietly, "I wouldn't let you do this if you weren't ready. You have to trust me. And trust yourself."

Kelly shrugged, then slowly she mounted the beam.

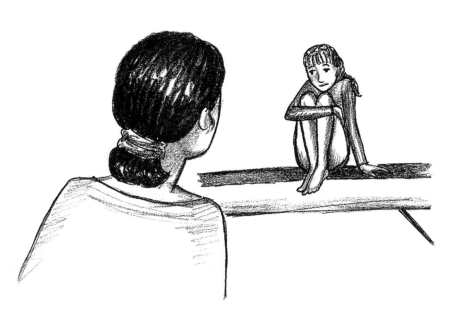

She took a breath and raised her arms. Nadia was spotting for her. She was standing beside the beam to support her if she needed help. Kelly's chest felt tight. She forced herself to ignore it.

She leapt backward. Nadia's hands lightly touched her back. Kelly's hands hit the beam, and her legs followed. She tried to make it stick by raising her head and holding her arms up like she was taught.

"Fight for your landing!" Nadia yelled.

But Kelly didn't fight.

Instead of holding the lunge position, she let herself fall onto the mat.

"You did the handspring," said Nadia, "but then you gave up. Why?"

"I don't know," said Kelly.

"You don't have time to give up. You have to stick it. You have to make it stick a hundred times before you can do it well in the championships."

Kelly nodded. She knew what it would take.

Chapter 4
Practice! Practice! Practice!

Every day, Kelly arrived at the gym early and left later than the other girls.

"Run harder," Nadia would yell. Kelly, each day, pushed herself to be faster in her run up to the vaulting horse.

"Higher," her coach would say as they worked on her floor routine. Soon, Kelly's aerials were higher.

"Straighter in the handstand," Kelly reminded herself, and everything from her arms to her toes would tighten.

Soon, she could almost manage a perfect back handspring on the beam.

"Better," Nadia would growl, "but you're still hesitating at the start."

"I'll try it again," Kelly would say. And she did, over and over again until her body knew exactly what to do.

At the same time, Kelly trained her mind. As she stood beside the beam, she imagined her body flipping perfectly. She would shake her arms to get rid of her nerves. She would not let herself think about what could go wrong.

Chapter 5
The Accident

One week before the competition, Kelly stayed late to do some extra practice on the beam.

"Good work," Nadia called from the other side of the gym. "Excellent! Now take a rest."

Kelly grinned. "One more?"

"OK," said Nadia, "one more."

Kelly raised her arms over her head.

She closed her eyes for just a second. Suddenly, a picture formed in her mind. She saw the girl and her broken ankle. Kelly tried to erase the thought.

"I should just go home," she said to herself.

But Kelly didn't want to.

"Just one more time," she thought.

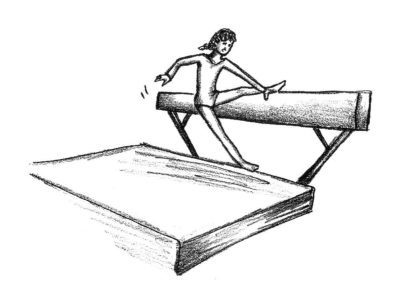

Without clearing her mind, she leapt off the beam into the air. Her back curved. Her arms swung over her head.

She landed, but her arms weren't straight enough. Her legs flipped over her body, but her right foot slipped off the beam. She fell onto the mat.

Pain shot through her foot. Her body fell to the ground.

"Kelly!" Nadia yelled as she ran to her side.

Kelly gripped her ankle.

"I'm OK," she said, but a huge lump formed in her throat.

"You don't look OK," Nadia said, helping Kelly to a chair. "We're going to the hospital right away."

Chapter 6
A Lucky Escape

The badge on the doctor's coat read "Dr. Wendy Baker."

"Well, it's not broken," she said. Kelly sighed with relief. "It's going to be sore for awhile," the doctor continued. "No gymnastics, I'm afraid."

Kelly's eyes widened in panic.

"What? How long?" she said. "I've got a competition next week."

"Only a couple of days," said Dr. Baker. "Don't worry, Kelly. You should be OK for your competition."

"But you don't understand. I need to keep training. I can't stop now!" Kelly cried.

"Kelly, if you don't rest this ankle, you won't be able to compete at all. It's as simple as that," Dr. Baker said.

Kelly opened her mouth to argue, but instead she burst into tears.

Chapter 7
Doctor's Orders

Kelly followed the doctor's orders. In training she worked only on her arms and stomach. She did push-ups, sit-ups, and pull-ups. Slowly, her foot began to feel better. On the morning of the competition, it was stiff, but the pain was gone.

As she warmed up with the other gymnasts, Kelly's fear grew. She had fallen off the beam. She could have broken her ankle. She hadn't been able to practice. What if she fell in front of the judges and scored badly? Or worse?

Kelly shook her head and tried not to think about anything worse.

"You've done the work, Kelly," Nadia said. "I know you can do this."

Kelly nodded. Her face was grim.

"You don't have to go through with it," Nadia added. "You could just swap it for a back walkover."

"But I won't score as well, and I'll never move up to Level Eight," said Kelly.

Another thought nagged at the back of her mind, too.

She knew her friends at the club had fears. All gymnasts do. Her friend Casey was scared of a somersault off the vaulting horse. Melissa didn't like to dismount from the high bar. To be a champion, you had to put fear aside.

"It takes guts," she said to herself.

She ran over to her father, who was sitting in the front row with the parents of the other kids in the club.

"What should I do, Dad?" she asked.

Her dad smiled.

"It's simple, Kell," he said. "Just do what you know you can do."

Chapter 8
I Can Do It!

Kelly stood beside the beam waiting for the judge's signal. She pushed everything out of her mind: the crowd, her ankle, the judges, the noise. When a tingle of fear began in her stomach, she pushed that out, too. Instead, she repeated her father's words in her mind: "Do what you know you can do."

The judge's signal came. She knew what she could do. She began with a handstand mount onto the beam, then a walkover. Her foot was numb as she stepped into a split change leap, then a full turn. In seconds, it was time—the back handspring.

"I can do it," she told herself.

She lifted her arms. Her feet sprang automatically. They pushed her high above the beam.

Her back curved. Her hands landed perfectly, but only for a second.

She flipped onto her feet in the lunge position. Her body wobbled a little, but not for long.

Kelly's arms shot up, and she raised her head to "mark it," which showed that her landing was strong and tight.

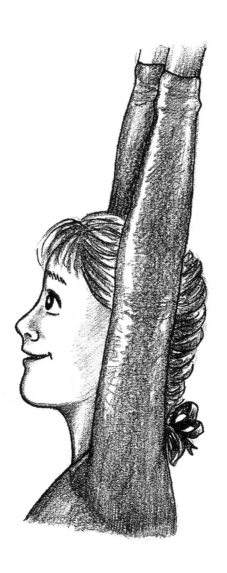

Kelly began to smile as she completed the routine. She dismounted with a perfect backward somersault.

"That's my girl," her father yelled from the sidelines. "You did it!"

Kelly gazed into the cheering crowd. Then she began to laugh.

"I did it!" she said to herself. "I did it!"

She ran into Nadia's arms.

"I did it, Nadia," she said.

Nadia hugged her.

"I knew you would. You're on your way now," Nadia said.

Chapter 9
A Good Score

Kelly didn't think much about the wobble. She knew it would cost her precious points, but she almost forgot to wait for her score.

"It's coming up," said Casey, pointing to the scoreboard.

And there it was—9.2. It was a good score, but not enough to win.

"Bummer," Casey shrugged, "but don't worry, Kell. Coming in second is pretty good, too."

Kelly laughed.

"No, Casey," she said, "coming in second is great!" She raced off to find her father in the crowd.

Chapter 10
Kelly Has the Last Word

Kelly's photo was in the paper again on Monday. This time it was on the back page. It was as small as a postage stamp.

As she walked into school, Kelly heard a familiar voice.

"Oh, look everyone," the voice said. "Here comes 'Tomorrow's Olympian!'"

Kelly stopped walking. It was Annabelle. She felt her stomach flutter.

"Guts," she said to herself. "I HAVE the guts." She closed her eyes for a second and imagined how it felt to do the back handspring on the beam.

She opened her eyes and turned to face Annabelle ... Annabottom ... Spannerbelle ... Annasmell. Kelly began to giggle. She wasn't nervous anymore.

"Did you say 'Tomorrow's Olympian?'" Kelly asked. She held her head high. "Thanks, Annabelle! I hope you're right."

Before Annabelle could open her mouth again, Kelly turned her back and walked away, smiling.

The National Championship was coming up in a few months. She had more important things to think about.

Glossary

automatically—done without thinking

blurted—said quickly without thinking

ignore—refuse to notice

nagged—to keep complaining over and over again

precious—of great value

private—secret

Technical Terms

a natural—a person born with special abilities

aerials—cartwheels done without the hands touching the ground

balance beam—a long, narrow piece of wood covered with fabric or leather on which gymnasts balance; also called a beam

cartwheel—to tumble sideways, with arms and legs extended like the spokes of a wheel

dismount—to get off

floor routine—a series of movements done in a set time on a large mat, usually to music

gymnastics—specialized exercises

vaulting horse—a padded structure over which gymnasts jump; also called a vault

Gymnasium and Equipment

Gymnasium

Rings

Uneven Bars

Balance Beam

Vaulting Horse

Floor

Silk Ribbon

Artistic Gymnasts

Sleeveless Leotard

Leotard

Shorts

Rhythmic Gymnast

Female   Male

Basic Rules

There are two types of gymnastics:

1. Rhythmic gymnastics are for women only. Rhythmic gymnasts use hand apparatuses such as ribbons and balls.

2. Artistic gymnastics are for men and women. Artistic gymnastics include the rings, pommel horse, parallel bars, high bar, vaulting horse (vault), balance beam (beam), uneven bars, and floor exercises.

- Men compete in the following categories: the rings, pommel horse, parallel bars, high bar, vault, and floor exercises.

- Women compete in the following categories: vault, beam, uneven bars, and floor exercises.

- On the beam, gymnasts need to show elegance, flexibility, balance, and confidence.

- For their performance, gymnasts are scored on a scale of 10 (for example, 9.55), with 10 being the best. Points are taken off for any slight mistakes or falls.

Training Tips

Warm Up

Try running, jogging, skipping, hopping, and jumping.

Wear warm clothes such as a tracksuit.

Posture on the Beam

- feet turned out

- chest lifted up

- arms relaxed

- shoulders down

- head up

- neck long

- eyes focused on the end of the beam

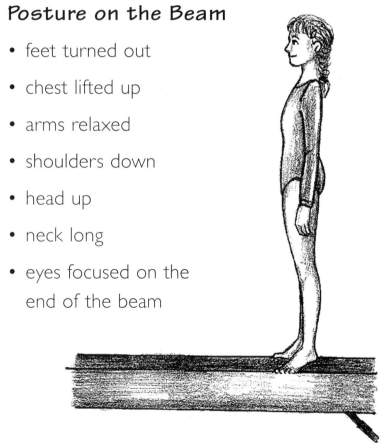

Flexibility

All muscles need to be regularly stretched so they are relaxed, or loose.

Flexibility helps prevent injuries.

Skill

The beam develops physical strength, agility, and mental focus.

Practice makes perfect.

Practice the movements on a low beam for safety.

Discipline

- Get rid of distractions.
- Overcome your fears.
- Feel in control.

Look for More
Read-it!
Chapter Books

Looking for a specific title?
A complete list of *Read-it!* Chapter Books
is available on our Web site:

www.picturewindowbooks.com